William's Wonderful Plan
and Other Stories

Richmal Crompton, who wrote the original *Just William* stories, was born in Lancashire in 1890. The first story about William Brown appeared in *Home* magazine in 1919, and the first collection of William stories was published in book form three years later. In all, thirty-eight William books were published, the last one in 1970, after Richmal Crompton's death.

Martin Jarvis, who has adapted the stories in this book for younger readers, first discovered *Just William* when he was nine years old. He made his first adaptation of a William story for BBC radio in 1973 and since then his broadcast readings have become classics in their own right. BBC Worldwide have released nearly a hundred William stories on audio cassette and for these international best-sellers Martin has received a Gold Disc and the British Talkies Award. An award-winning actor, Martin has also appeared in numerous stage plays, television series and films.

D0542170

All *Meet Just William* titles can be ordered at
your local bookshop or are available by post
from Book Service by Post (tel: 01624 675137).

William's Wonderful Plan and Other Stories

Adapted from Richmal Crompton's
original stories by Martin Jarvis

Illustrated by Tony Ross

MACMILLAN CHILDREN'S BOOKS

First published 1999 by Macmillan Children's Books
a division of Pan Macmillan Limited
20 New Wharf Road, London N1 9RR
Basingstoke and Oxford
www.panmacmillan.com

Associated companies throughout the world

ISBN 330 39102 X

A CIP catalogue record for this book is available from
the British Library.

Typeset by SX Composing DTP, Rayleigh, Essex
Printed and bound in Great Britain by Mackays of Chatham plc, Kent

Contents

Dear Reader

Ullo. I'm William Brown. Spect you've heard of me an' my dog Jumble cause we're jolly famous on account of all the adventures wot me an' my friends the Outlaws have.

Me an' the Outlaws try an' avoid our fam'lies cause they don' unnerstan' us. Specially my big brother Robert an' my rotten sister Ethel. She's awful. An' my parents are really <u>hartless</u>. Y'know, my father stops my pocket-money for no reason at all, an' my mother never lets me keep pet rats or <u>anythin'</u>.

It's jolly hard bein' an Outlaw an' havin' adventures when no one unnerstan's you, I can tell you.

You can read all about me, if you like, in this excitin' an' speshul new collexion of all my fav'rite stories. I hope you have a jolly gud time readin' 'em.

Yours truly

William Brown

William's Wonderful Plan

William noticed the caravan the first morning it appeared and formed his plans at once for acquaintance with its owners.

Caravans had a peculiar fascination for William. He had always found in caravan-dwellers, whether of gypsy or bohemian persuasion, a pleasing freedom from the conventions and prejudices of regular house-holders.

Immediately after school he made his way down to the caravan and hung about it. He could see a man in the next field seated at an easel, painting.

William was just about to draw closer to the caravan when a little girl appeared suddenly in the doorway. She was about William's age with a round, dimpled face and dark curls.

"What are you doing there, boy?" said the little girl in a clear voice. "Come and help me wash up."

Impressed despite himself by the imperiousness of the little girl's voice, William managed to preserve his manly independence so far as to reply, with a swaggering laugh, "Huh, you needn't try bossing me, 'cause I'm jolly well not goin' to be bossed by any ole girl."

But, even as he said it, he was turning to make his way meekly to the caravan, and within a few minutes was engaged in washing up and sweeping out the tiny room under the little girl's orders.

She informed him, while he did so, that she had had measles, and that this caravan holiday with her father was her final convalescence, before she returned to school.

2

"My father," she informed him, "is the greatest artist in the world. He can cook, too, but he's very untidy."

And she bustled about, dusting, tidying, putting away the tea things.

She was certainly not William's ideal caravan-dweller. On the other hand, her dimples were distinctly attractive, and William found her imperious manner intriguing.

After that, he called there regularly. He had become the little girl's willing slave. The artist addressed him vaguely as "boy" whenever he met him, and seemed to feel no curiosity about him.

William had told no one about the caravan and its occupants, but he soon found that the news had spread through the village.

Mrs Bott, of the Hall, coming to invite William to a children's garden party, added, "And I'm going to ask that little girl who's camping here with her father. He's quite distinguished, I hear. An RA and all that . . ."

When Mrs Bott had gone, William, who hated visits to the Hall, did his best to extricate himself from the festivity.

"I'm sure I shan't be well enough," he pleaded to his mother. "It's no good me goin' there with an illness comin' on, an' givin' it to everyone there."

"But you haven't got an illness, William," protested his mother.

"I din' say I'd got one jus' this minute. I only said I felt I was goin' to have one that afternoon. I mean it doesn't seem fair to people to say you'll go to a place when you *know* you're only goin' to give them all an illness."

"If you think you're going to be ill, William, I'll ask the doctor to call."

William beat a hasty retreat.

To his surprise, the little girl actually wanted to go to the party.

"Don't be silly, William," she said. "Of *course* I want to go. It's a *party*. The only thing is . . ."

She sighed and the sparkle died away from her face.

"Yes?" said William.

"I haven't got a proper party dress . . . I've just got an old muslin one, all washed out and ever so much too short . . . and all the others will have lovely dresses. I shan't enjoy it a bit . . ."

"Well, don't go then," said William.

She stamped her small foot. "Don't be *silly*. I tell you I *want* to go."

"Well, ask your father to get you a new dress."

"No, I won't. He's poor and he's working hard and he mustn't be worried. You see, the one I have does all right for school but it'll look *awful* at a garden party, because I *know* all the others will have nicer ones."

"Now, look here," said William impulsively, "don't you worry. I'll see that you have a nice party dress for it."

He was aghast when he heard himself make this astounding offer, but it was too late to retract. Her face beamed with joy.

"Oh, William! Will you *really*?"

He found her gratitude very pleasing.

"'Course I will," he said, with a short laugh. "A little thing like that's nothin' to me. Nothin' at all."

"But William, you mustn't let anyone know you're getting it for me, will you? I should feel like a beggar if you did."

William gave another short laugh.

"Oh, no," he said. "'Course I wouldn't do that. Oh no. I'll get you a jolly nice new party dress, a jolly nice new one. You needn't worry about *that*."

The little girl beamed once more.

"Oh, William!" she said. "You are wonderful."

"Mother," he said thoughtfully that evening. "I don't mind goin' to this party of Mrs Bott's, if I can go in fancy dress."

"But of *course* you can't go in fancy dress, William," said his mother firmly. "It isn't a fancy dress party."

"P'raps it is, and she forgot to say. Anyway, I think I ought to have a fancy dress ready, case it is."

"But William, what *nonsense*! And even if it is, you've got your Red Indian suit."

"I'm sick of that ole Red Indian suit. I want to go as a little girl. I want you to buy me a little girl's party dress, so that if we find it's fancy dress at the last minute, I can go in it."

"William, I can't think what's come over you."

"Nothin's come over me. Surely I can go to a fancy dress party as a little girl if I want to."

"But there is no fancy dress party," protested Mrs Brown again.

"Well, will you give me a little girl's party dress and count it my Christmas present?"

"No, William, no, and I've no time to stay here talking nonsense with you like this. I've got the lunch to see to."

William decided to approach the six-year-old Violet Elizabeth Bott in whose honour the garden party was being held.

He thought of the endless succession of elaborate frocks in which her small person made its appearance at all the local functions.

She was, of course, much smaller than the little girl of the caravan, but surely, thought William, the little girl could make one dress for herself out of two of Violet Elizabeth's.

He approached the Hall cautiously and found Violet Elizabeth sitting on an upturned wheelbarrow.

"I'm a princess, William," she announced with her habitual lisp. "An' you're my subject. You've got to bow when you speak to me."

Ordinarily, William would have ignored her, but to the lady's gratification and secret surprise he bowed.

"Look here," he began, "I want to ask you something."

"You must say 'Your Royal Highness' when you speak to me," said Violet Elizabeth imperiously.

"Your Royal Highness," muttered William. "Look here . . . I want to ask you—"

Violet Elizabeth had leapt from the wheel-barrow.

"I want to go for a ride," she said. "Make my throne into a chariot."

William obediently turned over the wheel-barrow.

"Now, look here," he said. "What I want to ask you—"

"Now you're my coachman," said Violet Elizabeth, reposing on the wheelbarrow and arranging her miniature skirt about her with dignity. "Give me a ride, coachman."

Still forcing his proud spirit to this uncon-genial servitude, William took up the handles of the wheelbarrow, and began to push the small tyrant round the lawn.

"Now, look here," he began again rather breathlessly. "This is what I wanted to ask you—"

"You must say 'Your Royal Highness' when you speak to me," said Violet Elizabeth. "If you don't, I'll have your head chopped off for treason. And go faster!"

"Your Royal Highness," said William. "Now this is what I wanted to ask you—"

"I'm having a new frock from London for our party," announced Violet Elizabeth.

It was a heaven-sent opening.

"I say," panted William, "you've got lots of party frocks, haven't you?"

"Hundreds an' hundreds, an' say 'Your Royal Highness' or I'll have you arrested for treason."

"Your Royal Highness – well now, suppose there was another little girl—"

Violet Elizabeth's interest was suddenly aroused.

"Yes. Go on."

"Suppose there was another little girl that was invited to your party, but had only got a very old frock to come in, wouldn't you want to give her some of your old party frocks so that she can have a nice one to come in?"

A seraphic smile appeared upon Violet Elizabeth's angel countenance.

"No, I wouldn't," she said. "I'd *like* her to come in an old frock, 'cause it would make my new frock seem smarter than ever."

There was only one thing to do and William did it. He tipped the young autocrat urgently out of the wheelbarrow on the lawn, then set off himself quickly down the drive.

For a second, fury and amazement deprived Violet Elizabeth of the power of speech. Then it returned and scream after shrill scream rent the peaceful summer morning.

William was slowly approaching the caravan. He had almost decided to admit failure, but when the little girl came running across the field to him he could not find it in his heart to disappoint her.

"Oh, William," she cried excitedly. "Have you got it?"

"Er – not yet," said William, trying rather unsuccessfully to assume an airy manner. "There's plenty of time."

"You have got a plan, haven't you, William?" she said, anxiously.

He laughed a carefree laugh that rang slightly hollow.

"'Course I have," he said. "I should jolly well think I've got a plan all right."

They reached the caravan, and he followed her into it. A much-washed white muslin dress lay over a chair. The little girl held it up.

"It looks *awful*," she said sorrowfully. "I'd rather go in it than not go at all, of course, but

I shall feel dreadful if I have to wear it. It's all washed to bits and it's miles too small. But – you *have* promised to get me a new one, haven't you, William?"

"Oh yes," said William with a ghastly smile. "Oh yes, don't you worry about that."

The church clock struck five. She flung the dress over the chair again.

"That's tea-time. I'd better go and fetch Father. Be an angel, William, and put on the kettle. The water's in the petrol tin, you know."

She ran off across the field and William, heavy-hearted, lit the spirit-lamp as he had seen the little girl do, and filled the kettle from the petrol tin.

He had often seen the little girl fill the kettle from the petrol tin, but he had never realised that the caravan contained two petrol tins, one full of water, the other of paraffin, and it was from the paraffin tin that William had filled the kettle.

The next few moments were like the climax

of a nightmare. As he placed the kettle on the spirit stand a sheet of flame burst out, precipitating him through the caravan door and on to the grass outside.

Through a whirligig of stars, he saw two men who happened to be passing leap into the caravan and fling their coats upon the bright sheet of flame.

The flame died down. Through eddies of smoke William, sitting with a blackened face and singed hair upon the grass, saw the scorched remnants of the little girl's dress,

now about the size of a pocket handkerchief, still reposing on the chair.

He gazed at it for a few moments, sprang to his feet, and fled from the scene of ruin.

For the next few days he felt as if he were still living in a nightmare. He dare not revisit the little girl; his brain seemed to be numbed and stupefied by the immensity of the catastrophe.

The day of the garden party arrived. He could think of nothing but the little girl, deprived by his act of the party to which she had been looking forward.

She had said that she would rather go in the old muslin dress than not go at all. And he had burnt the old muslin dress.

He walked slowly and in a hangdog fashion towards the Hall. The little girl would not be at the party, of course, but suppose she were waiting outside to reproach him . . .

He entered the gate, and crossed over the lawn to a group of little boys and gaily dressed little girls.

Suddenly he heard a cry of "William", and to his amazement he saw the little girl detach herself from the group and come across the lawn to him. She wore a very pretty and obviously new dress of pale pink.

"Oh, *William*," she was saying, "you are *wonderful*! Oh, William, thank you so much. It was so clever of you, and I'm so sorry that I didn't really believe you'd got a plan. And it was such a *wonderful* plan."

William was gazing at her, open-mouthed.

"W-w-w-w-what?" he demanded.

"Why, to burn my old dress so that the insurance people should give me a new one. They've given me a lovely new one, haven't they? Oh, William, it was so clever of you to think of it."

William recovered himself quickly. He assumed his easy swagger, smiling at her in affectionate condescension.

"Oh, that's all right," he said. "A little thing like that's nothin' to me."

Parrots for Ethel

"Now," said William to Douglas and Ginger, "'bout this animal lecture what I'm going to give. We'll have it in our summer-house, an' I'll lecture on 'em. An' we'll have all our cats and Jumble. And we'll colleck some more insecks, an' we'll have Ginger's dormouse."

"Right," said Ginger, "let's go and fetch the dormouse."

They passed the drawing-room where Ethel sat with George and Hector. George was Douglas's elder brother; Hector was Ginger's. Both young men were infatuated with Ethel.

"Douglas drove me half-mad with a beastly

19

mouth organ yesterday," groaned George, "till I took it from him and chucked it into the pond."

"Same here with Ginger's trumpet," said Hector.

"Well I'm sure no boy ever was half as bad as William," said Ethel with a sigh. "He broke a vase that was one of my greatest treasures yesterday with his bow and arrow. I confiscated them of course."

Both Hector and George made an inarticulate murmur of deep sympathy.

"And William had a thing," said Ethel dreamily, "that was supposed to sound like a bird chirping. Only it didn't. It went through and *through* my head."

"Oh what a *shame*," said Hector and George simultaneously, in passionate indignation.

"I'm very fond of birds," continued Ethel. "What sort do you like best?"

"I think that parrots are rather sweet," said Ethel. "Don't you?"

Neither spoke.

"I remember once," went on Ethel, "a friend of mine had to go into quarantine for measles, or something like that, and a friend of hers gave her a parrot to be comforting for her. He gave it in rather a nice way, too. He put it on the garden seat on the lawn, and sent in a letter to say that if she'd look out of her window she would see a little friend who had come to keep her company. Or something like that. She was always devoted to that parrot."

It was the next morning. Ethel was staring wildly at a letter she held in her hand.

"Daphne's got measles, and I was with her last night. Oh, what shall I do?"

"You'll have to go into quarantine, I'm afraid, dear," said her mother placidly.

William received the news without emotion. A more terrible tragedy had happened than Ethel's quarantine. Ginger's dormouse had died in the night.

Ginger and Douglas took the dead body to the summer-house, leaving William alone on the lawn, gloomily considering the prospect of his lecture thus deprived of its star turn.

He didn't at first see Ginger's brother Hector who had come round to the side of the house looking pale and distraught.

"This is terrible news," began Hector.

"Yes, isn't it?" said William. "Terrible."

"She seemed all right yesterday," continued Hector.

"She was, she was quite all right yesterday.

I think it was eatin' those berries."

"What berries?"

"Those berries Ginger gave her."

"Wha—? Did Ginger give her some berries?"

"Oh yes, all sorts of different coloured kinds of berries what he found about the garden and she ate them all."

"But I heard in the village it was measles."

"No, it's worse than measles. She's dead. She died in the night."

"*What?*"

"She's dead. When Ginger 'n' me came to clean out her cage this morning we found her dead."

"Clean out her c—? What the dickens are you talking about?"

"Our mouse," said William. "Weren't you?"

The visitor controlled himself with an effort.

"No. I was talking about your sister, Ethel."

"Oh, Ethel. Oh no. No, it's not measles, it's somethin' else. Quarantine or somethin'."

Hector turned on his heel and strode away. He'd remembered suddenly what Ethel had said. He'd get her a parrot.

William remained upon the garden bench, plunged in gloom. The voice of George broke upon his meditations.

"Well, I'm very sorry to hear this," began George.

William's heart warmed to him. Here, at any rate, was sympathy.

"Yes," he said. "Yes, it was an awful shock to us all to find her dead this mornin'."

"*What?*"

Explanation followed, and George walked quickly down the road. He'd suddenly remembered what Ethel had said about the parrot yesterday. He'd get her one.

William rejoined the others in the summer-house.

"Tell you what. We'll put up a notice asking people to lend us an'mals, or give us an'mals, like what they do to the zoo."

Ten minutes later they gathered round to look at William's notice. It read as follows:

"mister william brown is going to leckcher on anmals and will be gratful to anyone who will give or lend him anmals to be leckchered on mister william brown is out now lookin for valubul insex, but will be back before dinner mister william brown will be glad if people givin him anmals to be leckchered on will put them on the seat in the back garden an tie them up if they are savvidge anmals mister william brown's vallubul assistunts are ginger and douglas."

They pinned the notice on the side gate and sallied forth in search of insects.

A short time before their return, Hector appeared looking very hot and breathless. He held a parrot in a cage.

He had cycled frenziedly into the nearest town and had spent practically his last penny on it. He found a garden seat conveniently situated.

He then slipped a letter quietly through the
letter box. In the letter he said that if she
would look out of the window, she would see
upon the garden seat a little friend who had
come to keep her company.

Then, smiling fatuously to himself, he tip-
toed away.

Hardly had he disappeared, when the
Outlaws returned. They had found only one
species of caterpillar.

They turned the corner of the house, and
there upon the garden seat was a parrot in a

cage. They rushed to it and bore it off in triumph to the summer-house.

The parrot uttered a shrill scream of laughter, and said with deep feeling, "Go away, I hate you."

"Wonder what they eat?" said Ginger.

"I say, where's that tin with my caterpillar in?" said William. "Who's took it?"

"You left it on the garden seat, when we fetched the parrot in," said Douglas.

They hurried out to the garden seat.

It was empty.

Meanwhile, a housemaid had found Hector's note on the mat and taken it up to Ethel's room. Ethel's room did not happen to overlook the garden. She read the note with a smile, almost as fatuous as Hector's.

"A little friend to keep you company." Oh, it was very, very sweet of him. She opened the door, and called to the housemaid.

"Emma, will you bring me something that you'll find upon the garden seat."

Emma went out and returned with a small

tin. Inside were several leaves and a big furry caterpillar.

"Oh, *that's* his idea of being funny, is it?" said Ethel viciously. "Well, it's not *mine*."

And she flung the tin furiously into the fire-place.

At that very moment, the faithful George was tiptoeing softly round the side of the house, bearing a parrot in a cage, and the Outlaws were returning from another cater-pillar expedition.

"Funny we only caught one of those caterpillars again," said William.

"Well, one's enough to lecture on, I sup-pose," said Douglas.

William had stopped suddenly, and was staring in blank amazement.

"There – there's another parrot on the seat. Look. It is, isn't it? It *is* another parrot, isn't it?"

"Yes," said Ginger, "it cert'nly is. Seems sort of funny they should *all* be givin' us parrots, don't it?"

They took it into the summer-house, and the other parrot greeted it with a sardonic laugh. The latecomer gazed round with a supercilious air, and finally screamed, "Great Scott."

Then William said, "Where's that tin with the caterpillar in?"

"You left it on the bench again, William," said Douglas.

They went out and stood around the empty bench.

"*Well*," said William, "it's mos' *mysterious*. Someone's pinched this one too."

Upstairs Ethel was hurling the second caterpillar and tin furiously into the fireplace.

It was late afternoon. Hector, still wearing his fatuous smile, came round the corner of the house. He felt that he couldn't wait a minute longer without hearing an account of Ethel's rapturous glee on the receipt of his present.

A housemaid opened the door.

"I just called to see if the parrot was settling down all right," said Hector.

"The parrot?"

"Yes. The parrot that arrived this morning."

"No parrot arrived this morning, sir."

"W-what? Are you sure?"

"Oh quite sure, sir. There's no parrot in the house at all."

"Not – er – not in Miss Brown's room?"

"Oh no, sir. I've just been there."

Dazedly, Hector walked away. Then he

stopped. There, just outside the closed door of the summer-house, stood William with a parrot in a cage.

The two parrots had begun to hold a screaming contest, till William was forced to take George's outside.

Hector's first impulse was to hurl himself upon William and accuse him of stealing his parrot, but on approaching nearer he saw that it was not his parrot, and it was not his cage.

"Whose is that parrot, William?" he asked pleasantly.

"Mine," said William.

"W-where did you get it?" said Hector still more pleasantly.

"Someone gave it to me."

There was a short silence.

Then Hector said, "I'm – I'm willing to buy that parrot from you, William."

A sudden gleam had come into William's eye.

"I tell you what I'll do. I'll swap it with you."

"What for?" said Hector hopefully.

"I want to give Ginger a present. One of those nice trumpets. You can get them at Foley's in the village. They cost six shillings. I'll swap it with you for one of those trumpets to give to Ginger."

For a minute there was murder in Hector's eye, then he gulped and said, "Very well. You wait here."

Soon he was back with the trumpet. He hurled it at William, seized the parrot cage and disappeared. He was going to write a beautiful little note, fasten it to the cage, and deliver it in person at the front door.

Inside the summer-house the Outlaws were dancing a dance of exultation around Ginger, who was producing loud but discordant strains from his magnificent new trumpet.

This festive gathering was, however, broken by the sudden advent of George. Like Hector, he'd been informed that no parrot had entered the house that day.

He then caught a glimpse of the Outlaws in

the summer-house, leaping wildly about a parrot in a cage.

"You little *thieves*," he panted. "What do you *mean* by taking my parrot?"

"'S not your parrot, 's ours."

George looked at the parrot. William was right. It wasn't his cage. He gulped. He began to make tentative enquiries as to the exact value William set upon his parrot.

It appeared that William was willing to exchange it for a mouth organ, one of the six shilling ones from Foley's, because he wanted to give one to Douglas as a present.

George went off furiously to buy the mouth organ, returned with it, flung it at the Outlaws and stalked off with his parrot.

At a discreet distance, the Outlaws followed George round and out of the side gate. George was going to take the parrot in at the front door, ring the bell, and deliver it in person.

And then, to his amazement, he saw Hector blithely approaching from the opposite direction, also carrying a parrot in a cage.

They met at the gate. Each recognised his own parrot and cage in the hand of the other.

Simultaneously they shouted, "So *you* stole my parrot!"

The Outlaws watched in mystified delight. A shabby-looking man who happened to be passing also stopped to form an interested audience.

George turned round, thrust the cage into William's arms with a curt, "Take that", and began to roll up his sleeves.

Hector turned to the shabby-looking man, thrust his cage into his arms, and the next minute, George and Hector were giving a splendid boxing display upon the high road with bare fists.

The shabby man crept softly away with his parrot and cage. Very thoughtfully, William carried his cage up to Ethel's room.

"Erm, I won't come in, Ethel," he said, "'cause of catching your quarantine illness, but I've brought you a little present. I heard you said you'd like a parrot, and I brought you one."

Ethel was deeply touched. "How very kind of you, William," she said. "I – er – you can have your bow and arrow back. I'm sorry I took it from you. It's very kind of you to bring me the parrot."

Willliam received his bow and arrow with perfunctory thanks. Just at that moment the housemaid came up with a note. Ethel tore it open.

"Why, it's all right," she said. "Daphne hasn't got measles after all. The rash has all gone. And the doctor said she's not got it at all. And they want me to go to tea. And they've got that handsome artist coming. Oh, how jolly. I'll start at once."

A few minutes later, Ethel, accompanied by William, Ginger and Douglas, set out from the front door. At the gate Hector and George came forward to greet them.

The fight was just over, abandoned by mutual consent. Ethel passed them head in air. They stood, gaping after her in helpless bewilderment.

The Outlaws turned back to look at them. Ginger and Douglas raised trumpet and mouth organ to their lips and uttered defiant strains. William waved his bow and arrow in careless greeting.

They had had a most successful day. There had been, it's true, certain mysterious elements in it that they couldn't understand, but that didn't matter. They were perfectly happy.

The Bishop's Handkerchief

Until now William had taken no interest in his handkerchiefs as accessories. But last week, Ginger (a member of the circle known to themselves as the Outlaws, of which William was the leader) had received a handkerchief as a birthday present from an aunt in London.

William, on hearing the news, had jeered, but the sight of the handkerchief had silenced him. It was a large handkerchief, larger than William had conceived it possible for handkerchiefs to be. It was made of silk, and contained all the colours of the rainbow.

Round the edge, green dragons sported upon a red ground.

Ginger displayed it, fully prepared for scorn and merriment, but there was something about the handkerchief that impressed them all . . .

The next morning Henry appeared with a handkerchief almost exactly like it, and the day after that Douglas had one. William felt his prestige lowered. He – the born leader – was the only one of the select circle who did not possess a coloured silk handkerchief.

That evening he approached his mother.

"I don't think white ones is much use," he said.

"Don't scrape your feet on the carpet, William," said his mother placidly. "I thought white ones were the only tame kind – not that I think your father will let you have any more. You know what he said when they got all over the floor and bit his finger."

"I'm not talkin' about *rats*," said William. "I'm talkin' about handkerchiefs."

"Oh – handkerchiefs! White ones are far the best. There's nothing better than white linen."

"Pers'nally," said William with a judicial air, "I think silk's better than linen, an' white's so tirin' to look at. I think a kind of colour's better for your eyes. My eyes do ache a bit sometimes. I think it's prob'ly with keep lookin' at white handkerchiefs."

"Don't be silly, William. I'm not going to

buy you silk handkerchiefs to get covered with mud and ink and coal, as yours do . . ."

William decided to investigate Robert's bedroom. He opened Robert's dressing-table drawer and turned over the handkerchiefs.

He caught his breath with surprise and pleasure. There, beneath all Robert's other handkerchiefs, was a larger, silkier, more multi-coloured handkerchief than Ginger's or Douglas's or Henry's.

He gazed at it in ecstatic joy. He slipped it into his pocket and, standing before the looking glass, took it out with a flourish, shaking its lustrous folds.

He was absorbed in this occupation when Robert entered.

"What do you think *you're* doing?"

"Oh, I jus' wanted to borrow a handkerchief, Robert. I thought you wun't mind lendin' me this handkerchief."

"Well, I would," said Robert curtly. "Give it back to me."

Reluctantly William handed it back to Robert.

"How much'll you give it me for?" he said.

"Well, how much have you?" said Robert, ruthlessly.

"Nothin' – jus' at present," admitted William. "But I'd *do* something for you for it. I'd do anythin' you want done for it. You just tell me what to do for it, an' I'll *do* it."

"Well, you can – you can get the Bishop's handkerchief for me, and then I'll give mine to you."

The trouble with Robert was that he imagined himself a wit.

The trouble with William was that he took things literally.

The Bishop was expected in the village the next day. It was the great event of the summer. He was a distant relation of the Vicar's.

He was to open the Fête, address a large meeting on Temperance, spend the night at the vicarage, and depart the next morning.

The Bishop was a fatherly, simple-minded old man of seventy. He enjoyed the Fête, except for one thing. Wherever he looked, he met the gaze of a freckled untidy frowning small boy.

He could not understand it. The boy seemed to be everywhere. The boy seemed to follow him about . . .

Then he addressed the meeting on Temperance, his audience consisting chiefly of adults. But in the front seat, the same earnest frowning boy fixed him with a determined gaze . . .

After the meeting William wandered down the road to the Vicarage. He pondered gloomily over his wasted afternoon. Fate had not thrown the Bishop's handkerchief in his path. But he did not yet despair.

He looked cautiously through the Vicarage hedge. Nothing was to be seen. He crawled inside the garden and round to the back of the house. The Bishop was tired after his address. He lay outstretched upon a deckchair beneath a tree.

Over the head and face of His Lordship, was stretched a large super-fine linen hand-kerchief. William's set expression brightened. On hands and knees he began to crawl through the grass, towards the portly form.

Crouching behind the chair, he braced him-self for the crime; he measured the distance between the chair and the garden gate.

One, two, three – then suddenly the portly form stirred, the handkerchief was firmly withdrawn by a podgy hand, and a dignified voice yawned and said, "Heigh-ho!"

At the same moment the Bishop sat up. William, from his refuge behind the chair, looked wildly round. The door of the house was opening. There was only one thing to do.

William was as nimble as a monkey. Like a flash of lightning he disappeared up a tree. It was a very leafy tree. It completely concealed William, but William had a good bird's eye view of the world beneath him.

The Vicar came out rubbing his hands.

"You rested, my Lord?" he said.

"I'm afraid I've had forty winks," said His Lordship pleasantly. "Just dropped off, you know. I dreamt about that boy who was at the meeting this afternoon."

"What boy, my Lord?" asked the Vicar.

"I noticed him at the Fête and the meeting. He looked – he looked a soulful boy. I dare say you know him."

The Vicar considered.

"I can't think of any boy round here like that," he said.

The Bishop sighed.

"It seemed an earnest *questing* face – as if the boy wanted something – *needed* something. I hope my little talk helped him."

"Without doubt it did, my Lord," said the Vicar, politely. "I thought we might dine out here – the days draw out so pleasantly now."

The Vicar went to order dinner in the garden. The Bishop drew the delicate handkerchief once more over his rubicund features.

The breast of the Bishop on the lawn began to rise and sink. The figure of the Vicar was visible at the study window, as he gazed with fond pride upon the slumbers of his distinguished guest.

William dared not descend in view of that watching figure. Finally, it sat down in a chair by the window, and began to read a book.

William took from his pocket a bent pin attached to a piece of string. This apparatus lived permanently in his pocket, because he had not given up hope of catching a trout in the village stream.

He lowered this cautiously and drew the bent pin carefully on the white linen expanse.

Leaning down from his leafy retreat, William drew the bent pin sharply across. It missed the handkerchief and caught the Bishop's ear.

The Bishop sat up with a scream. William, pin and string withdrew into the shade of the branches.

The Vicar ran out from the house, full of concern.

"I've been badly stung in the ear by some insect," said the Bishop. "Some virulent tropical insect, I should think – very painful. Very painful indeed—"

"My Lord," said the Vicar. "I am so sorry – so very sorry – a thousand pardons – can I procure some remedy for you – vaseline, ammonia – er – cold cream—?"

"No, no, no, no," snapped the Bishop. "I put my handkerchief over my face for a protection. If I had failed to do that I should have been even more badly stung."

The Vicar sat himself down on his chair.

The maid came out to lay the table. They watched her in silence. William shifted his position in the tree.

"Do you know," said the Bishop, "I believe that there is a cat in the tree. Several times I have heard a slight rustling."

It would have been better for William to

remain silent, but William's genius occasion-ally misled him. He was anxious to prevent the investigation; to prove once and for all his identity as a cat.

He leant forward and uttered a re-echoing "Mi-*aw-aw-aw!*"

As imitations go, it was rather good.

There was a slight silence. Then, "It *is* a cat," said the Bishop in triumph.

"Excuse me, my Lord," said the Vicar.

He went softly into the house and returned holding a shoe.

"This will settle his feline majesty," he smiled.

Then he hurled the shoe violently into the tree.

"Sh! Scoot!" he said as he did it.

William was annoyed. The shoe narrowly missed his face. He secured it and waited.

"I hope you haven't lost the shoe," said the Bishop anxiously.

"Oh, no. The gardener's boy will get it for me."

He settled himself in his chair comfortably with a smile.

William leant down, held the shoe deliberately over the Vicar's bald head then dropped it.

"*Damn!*" said the Vicar. "Excuse me, my Lord."

"H'm," said the Bishop. "Er – yes – most annoying. It lodged in a branch for a time probably, and then obeyed the force of gravity."

The Vicar was rubbing his head. William wanted to enjoy the sight of the Vicar rubbing his head. He moved a little further along the branch.

He forgot all caution. There was the sound of a rending and a crashing, and on to the table between the amazed Vicar and Bishop descended William's branch and William.

The Bishop gazed at him. "Why, that's the boy," he said.

William sat up among the debris of broken glass and crockery. He discovered that he was

bruised and that his hand was cut by one of the broken glasses.

He extricated himself from the branch and the table, and stood rubbing his bruises and sucking his hand.

"Crumbs!" was all he said.

The Vicar was gazing at him speechlessly.

"You know, my boy," said the Bishop in mild reproach, "that's a very curious thing to do – to hide up there for the purpose of eaves-dropping.

"I know that you are an earnest, well-meaning little boy, and that you were inter-ested in my address this afternoon, and I dare say you were hoping to listen to me again, but this is my time for relaxation, you know.

"Suppose the Vicar and I had been talking about something we didn't want you to hear? I'm sure you wouldn't like to listen to things people didn't want you to hear, would you?"

William stared at him in unconcealed amazement.

The Vicar, with growing memories of shoes

and "damns" and with murder in his heart, was picking up twigs and broken glass.

He knew that he could not, in the Bishop's presence, say the things to William and do the things to William that he wanted to do and say.

He contented himself with saying, "You'd better go home now. Tell your father I'll be coming to see him tomorrow."

"A well-meaning little boy, I'm sure," said the Bishop kindly. "Well-meaning, but unwise – er – unwise. But your attentiveness during the meeting did you credit, my boy – did you credit."

William turned to go. He knew when he was beaten. He had spent a lot of time and trouble and had not secured the episcopal handkerchief. He had bruised himself and cut himself.

He understood the Vicar's veiled threat. He saw all his future pocket-money vanish into nothingness with the cost of the Vicar's glasses and plates.

He wouldn't have minded if he'd got the handkerchief. He wouldn't have minded anything if—

"Don't suck your hand, my boy," said the Bishop. "An open cut like that is most dangerous. Poison works into the system by it. You remember I told you how the poison of alcohol works into the system – well, any kind of poison can work into it by a cut – don't suck it; keep it covered up – haven't you a handkerchief? Here, take mine. You needn't trouble to return it. It's an old one."

The Bishop was deeply touched by what he called the "bright spirituality" of the smile with which William thanked him.

William, limping slightly, his hand covered by a grimy rag, came out into the garden, drawing from his pocket with a triumphant flourish an enormous, violently-coloured silk handkerchief.

Robert, who was weeding the rose-bed, looked up.

"Here," he called, "you can jolly well go and put that handkerchief of mine back."

William continued his proud advance.

"'S all right," he called airily, "the Bishop's is on your dressing-table."

Robert dropped his trowel.

"Gosh!" he gasped, and hastened indoors to investigate.

William went down to the gate, smiling very slightly.

"The days are drawing out so pleasantly," he was saying to himself in a mincing accent.

"Vaseline – ammonia – er – or cold cream. Damn!"

He leant over the gate and looked up and down the road. In the distance he caught sight of the figure of his friend.

"Gin-*ger*," he yelled in hideous shrillness.

He waved his coloured handkerchief carelessly in greeting as he called. Then he swaggered out into the road . . .

William and St Valentine

Miss Lomas held a Bible class for the Sons and Daughters of Gentlefolk every Tuesday afternoon after school. Something seemed to have happened to the class since William Brown joined it. The beautiful atmosphere was destroyed.

William took his seat in the dining-room where Miss Lomas always held her class. He took a large nut out of his pocket and cracked it with his teeth.

"*Not* in here, William," said Miss Lomas faintly.

"I was goin' to put the bits of shell into my

61

pocket," said William. "I wasn't goin' to put 'em on your carpet or anything; but 'f you don't want me to 's all right," he said obligingly, putting nut and dismembered shell into his pocket.

"Now," said Miss Lomas brightly, "I want to give you a little talk on Brotherly Love."

"Who's St Valentine?" said William who was burrowing in his prayer book.

"Why, William?" said Miss Lomas, patiently.

"Well, his day seems to be comin', this month," said William.

Miss Lomas, with a good deal of confusion, launched into a not very clear account of the institution of St Valentine's Day.

"Well, I don't think much of *him* 's a saint," was William's verdict, "writin' soppy letters to girls instead of gettin' martyred prop'ly like Peter an' the others."

Miss Lomas put her hand to her head.

"You misunderstand me, William," she said. "What I meant to say was . . . Well, suppose we leave St Valentine till later, and have our little talk on Brotherly Love first . . . *Ow-w-w!*"

The box containing William's pet stag-beetle, Albert, had accidentally opened in William's pocket, and Albert was now taking a voyage of discovery up Miss Lomas's jumper. Miss Lomas's spectacles fell off. She tore Albert off her and rushed from the room.

William gathered up his stag-beetle and carefully examined him.

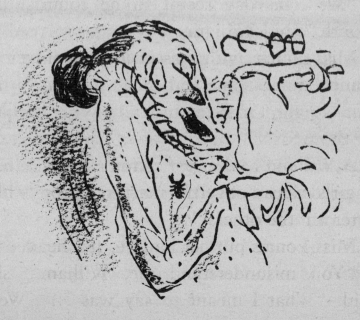

"She might have hurt him, throwing him about like that," he said sternly. "She oughter be more careful."

Then he replaced Albert tenderly in his box.

At that moment, Miss Dobson entered the room. Miss Dobson was Miss Lomas's cousin and was staying with her. Miss Dobson was very young and very pretty. She had short golden curls and blue eyes and small white teeth and an attractive smile.

"My cousin's not well enough to finish the lesson," she said. "So, I'm going to read to you all till it's time to go home. Now, let's be comfortable. Come and sit on the hearthrug. That's right. I'm going to read to you 'Scalped by the Reds'."

At the end of the first chapter, William had decided that he wouldn't mind coming to this sort of Bible class every day.

At the end of the second he had decided to marry Miss Dobson as soon as he grew up . . .

*

When William woke up the next morning, his determination to marry Miss Dobson was unchanged.

He had previously agreed quite informally to marry Joan Parfitt, his friend and play-mate and adorer, but Joan was small and dark-haired and rather silent. She was not gloriously grown-up, and tall and fair and vivacious.

William was aware that marriage must be preceded by courtship, and that courtship was an arduous business.

It was a half-holiday that afternoon and, to the consternation of his family, William announced his intention of staying at home.

He knew that Laurence Hinlock, Ethel's latest admirer, was expected for tea and William wished to study at near quarters the delicate art of courtship.

He realised that he could not marry Miss Dobson for many years to come, but he did not see why his courtship of her should not begin at once . . . He was going to learn how it was done from Laurence Hinlock and Ethel . . .

He spent the earlier part of the afternoon collecting a few more insects for his empty boxes. (He was still mourning bitterly the loss of Albert, who had been confiscated that morning by the French master.)

Then he went indoors.

There were several people in the drawing-room. He greeted them rather coldly, his eye roving round the while for what he sought.

Ethel and a tall, lank young man were sitting in the window-alcove, in two comfortable chairs, talking vivaciously and confidentially.

William took a chair and carried it over to them, put it down by the young man's chair, and sat down.

There was a short, pregnant silence.

"Good afternoon," said William, at last.

"Er – good afternoon," said the young man.

There was another silence.

"Hadn't you better go and speak to the others?" said Ethel.

"I've spoke to them," said William.

Silence again.

"I think Mrs Franks would like you to go and talk to her," said Ethel.

"No, I don't think she would," said William with perfect truth.

The young man took out a shilling and handed it to William.

"Go and buy some sweets for yourself," he said.

William put the shilling in his pocket.

"Thanks," he said. "I'll go and get them when you've all gone."

There was another and yet deeper silence. Then Ethel and the young man began to talk together again.

They had evidently decided to ignore William's presence.

William listened with rapt attention. He wanted to know what you said and the sort of voice you said it in.

"St Valentine's Day next week," said Laurence soulfully.

"Oh, no one takes any notice of that nowadays," said Ethel.

"I'm going to," said Laurence. "I think it's a beautiful idea. Its meaning, you know . . . true love . . . If I send you a Valentine, will you accept it?"

"That depends on the Valentine," said Ethel with a smile.

"It's the thought that's behind it that's the vital thing," said Laurence. "It's that that matters. Ethel . . . you're in all my waking dreams."

"I'm sure I'm not," said Ethel.

"You are . . . Has anyone told you before that you're a perfect Botticelli?"

"Heaps of people," said Ethel calmly.

"I was thinking about love last night," said Laurence. "Love at first sight. That's the only sort of love . . . When I first saw you, my heart leapt at the sight of you."

Laurence was a great reader of romance.

"I think that we're predestined for each other. We must have known each other in former existences. We—"

"Do speak up," said William irritably. "You're speaking so low that I can't hear what you're saying . . ."

"What do people mean by sayin' they'll send a Valentine, Mother?" said William that evening. "I thought he was a sort of saint. I don' see how you can send a saint to anyone, 'specially when he's dead 'n' in the prayer book."

"Well, it's a kind of Christmas card," said Mrs Brown vaguely, "only it's a Valentine, I mean . . . well it had gone out in my day, but I remember your grandmother showing me some that had been sent to her . . . dried ferns and flowers pasted on cardboard . . . very pretty."

"Huh!" said William. "I don' see any sense in sendin' pasted ferns, an' dead saints and things . . . But still, I'm going to do all the sort of things they do."

"What *are* you talking about, William?" said Mrs Brown.

Interest in St Valentine's Day seemed to have infected the whole household. On February 13th, William came upon his brother Robert wrapping up a large box of chocolates.

"What's that?" said William.

"A Valentine," said Robert shortly.

"Well, Miss Lomas said it was a dead saint, and Mother said it was a pasted fern, an' now you start sayin' it's a box of chocolates! No

one seems to know what it is. Who's it for, anyway?"

"Doreen Dobson," said Robert, answering without thinking with a glorifying blush.

"Oh, I *say*!" said William indignantly. "You can't. I've bagged her. I'm going to do a fern for her. I've had her ever since Bible class."

"Shut up and get out," said Robert.

Robert was twice William's size. William shut up and got out.

*

The Lomas family was giving a party on Saint Valentine's Day and William had been invited with Robert and Ethel. William spent two hours on his Valentine.

He could not find a fern so he picked a large spray of yew-tree instead. He found a large piece of thick cardboard, about the size of a drawing-board, and a bottle of glue in the cupboard of his father's writing-desk.

It took the whole bottle of glue, plus some flour and water, to fix the spray of yew-tree to the cardboard, and the glue mingled freely with the flour and water on William's clothing and person.

Finally, he surveyed his handiwork.

"Well, I don't see much *in* it now it's done," he said. "But I'm jolly well going to do all the things they do."

He set off to Miss Lomas's carrying his Valentine under his arm. He started out before Ethel and Robert because he wanted to begin his courtship of Miss Dobson before anyone else was in the field.

Miss Lomas opened the door. She paled slightly as she saw William.

"You're rather early," she said.

"Yes, I thought I'd come early so's to be sure to be in time," said William. "Which room're we goin' to have tea in?"

With a gesture of hopelessness Miss Lomas showed him into the empty drawing-room.

"It's Miss Dobson I've really come for," explained William obligingly as he sat down.

Miss Lomas fled, but Miss Dobson did not appear.

William spent the interval wrestling with his Valentine. He had carried it sticky side towards his coat, and it now adhered closely to him.

He managed at last to tear it away, leaving a good deal of glue and bits of yew-tree still attached to the coat . . .

The guests began to arrive, Robert and Ethel among the first. Miss Dobson came in with Robert. He handed her a large box of chocolates.

"A Valentine," he said.

"Oh . . . thank you," said Miss Dobson, blushing.

William took up his enormous piece of gluey cardboard with bits of battered yew adhering at intervals.

"A Valentine," he said.

Miss Dobson looked at it in silence.

"W-what is it, William?" she said faintly.

"A Valentine," repeated William, annoyed at its reception.

"Oh," said Miss Dobson.

Robert led her over to the recess by the window, which contained two chairs. William followed, carrying his chair. He sat down beside them. Both ignored him.

"Quite a nice day, isn't it?" said Robert.

"Isn't it!" said Miss Dobson.

"Miss Dobson," said William, "I'm always dreamin' of you when I'm awake."

"What a pretty idea of yours to have a Valentine's Day party," said Robert.

"Do you think so?" said Miss Dobson coyly.

"Has anyone ever told you that you're like a bottled cherry?" said William doggedly.

"Do you know . . . this is the first Valentine I've ever given anyone?" said Robert.

"Oh . . . is it?" she said.

"I've been thinkin' about love at first sight," said William monotonously. "I got such a fright when I saw you first. I think we're pre-existed for each other. I—"

"Will you allow me to take you out in my side-car tomorrow?" said Robert.

"Oh, how lovely!" said Miss Dobson.

"No . . . predestinated . . . that's it," said William.

Neither of them took any notice of him. He felt depressed, and disillusioned. She wasn't much of a catch anyway. He didn't know why he'd even bothered about her.

He was quiet for a minute or two. Then he took up his Valentine which was lying on the floor, and walked out.

The Outlaws were in the old barn. They greeted William joyfully. Joan, the only girl member, was there with them. William handed her his cardboard.

"A Valentine," he said.

"A Valentine?" said Joan.

"Yes. Some say it's a saint what wrote soppy letters to girls an' some say it's a bit of fern like this an' some say it's a box of chocolates."

"Well, I never!" said Joan. "It's beautiful of you to give it to me, William."

"It's a jolly good piece of cardboard," said Ginger. "'F we scrape away these messy leaves an' stuff."

William joined with zest in the scraping.

"How's Albert?" said Joan.

After all, there was no one quite like Joan. He'd never contemplate marrying anyone else again.

"He's been took off me," said William.

"Oh, what a *shame*, William!"

"But I've got another . . . an earwig . . . called Fred."

"I'm so glad."

"But I like you better than *any* insect, Joan," he said generously.

"Oh, William, do you *really*?"

"Yes – an' I'm goin' to marry you when I grow up if you won't want me to talk a lot of soppy stuff that no one can understand."

"Oh, thank you, William . . . No, I won't."

"All right . . . now come on an' let's play Red Indians."

Meet Just William
Richmal Crompton
Adapted by Martin Jarvis
Illustrated by Tony Ross

Just William as you've never seen him before!

A wonderful new series of *Just William* books, each containing four of his funniest stories – all specially adapted for younger readers by Martin Jarvis, the famous "voice of William" on radio and best-selling audio cassette.

Meet Just William and the long-suffering Brown family, as well as the Outlaws, Violet Elizabeth Bott and a host of other favourite characters in these ten hilarious books.

Richmal Crompton
Just William at School

"School's not nat'ral at all," said William. "Still, I don't suppose they'd let us give it up altogether, 'cause of schoolmasters havin' to have somethin' to do."

School is fertile ground for a boy of William's infinite trouble-making talent. Especially when he'd rather not be there at all. Whether he's feigning illness to avoid a test, campaigning for the abolition of Latin and Arithmetic, or breaking into Ole Fathead's house in pursuit of justice, William brings muddle and mayhem to anyone who tries to teach him a lesson.

Ten classic stories of William at school – and trying desperately to get out of it!

Richmal Crompton
Just William on Holiday

"No one stops them *enjoying themselves," muttered William.*
"They go about havin' a good time all the time, but the minute
I *start they all get mad at me!"*

Holidays are supposed to be a time for rest and recreation.
But somehow none of the Brown family seem to spend much
time relaxing with William around!

Whether he's rescuing a damsel in distress, sailing the
high seas to discover an uncharted island, or capturing a
dangerous smuggler on the beach, William never fails to
turn his holidays into chaotic adventures that no one will
ever forget.

Collect all the titles in the
MEET JUST WILLIAM series!

The prices shown below are correct at the time of going to press. However, Macmillan Publishers reserve the right to show new retail prices on covers which may differ from those previously advertised.

William's Birthday and Other Stories	0 330 39097 X	£2.99
William and the Hidden Treasure and Other Stories	0 330 39100 3	£2.99
William's Wonderful Plan and Other Stories	0 330 39102 X	£2.99
William and the Prize Cat and Other Stories	0 330 39098 8	£2.99
William and the Haunted House and Other Stories	0 330 39101 1	£2.99
William's Day Off and Other Stories	0 330 39099 6	£2.99
William and the White Elephants and Other Stories	0 330 39210 7	£2.99
William and the School Report and Other Stories	0 330 39211 5	£2.99
William's Midnight Adventure and Other Stories	0 330 39212 3	£2.99
William's Busy Day and Other Stories	0 330 39213 1	£2.99
William the Great Actor and Other Stories	0 330 48373 0	£2.99
William and the Bomb and Other Stories	0 330 48374 9	£2.99

All *Meet Just William* titles can be ordered from our website, www.panmacmillan.com, or from your local bookshop and are available by post from:

Bookpost
PO Box 29, Douglas, Isle of Man IM99 1BQ
Credit cards accepted. For details:
Telephone: 01624 836000
Fax: 01624 670923
E-mail: bookshop@enterprise.net
www.bookpost.co.uk

Free postage and packing in the UK.